# CoW

## and the Christmas Surprise

New Kids Media™ is published by Baker Book House Company, P.O. Box 6287, Grand Rapids, MI 49516-6287

ISBN 0-8010-4517-7

Printed in China

1 2 3 4 5 6 7 – 06 05 04 03

Visit Cowontheweb.com

# CoW
## and the Christmas Surprise

*Todd Aaron Smith*

NEW
KIds
MEDiA

BAKER
A DIVISION OF
Baker Book House Co

Cow watched feathery snowflakes fall across the field as she looked for a warm spot to stand. Up the hill she saw a lone figure where all the children played earlier that day.

Cow decided the polite thing to do would be to introduce herself. She walked toward the still figure. "Hello, friend!" she called. "It sure is cold today."

But the figure didn't answer.

Cow tried again. "What I said was, 'It sure is cold today!'"

The mysterious figure still did not answer. It did not even move.

Pig heard Cow and squealed with laughter. "Ha ha! Oh Cow! Don't you know you're talking to a snowman?! Ha ha ha! The kids who played here earlier built it."

Cow's eyes got very big. "A person made of snow?" she asked slowly. Cow had never seen anything before like this.

"That's wonderful!" she said. "I want to make something out of snow!"

"Go ahead," Pig said. "There's lots of snow. You can build whatever you want."

"Well," Cow said, "if those children can build a snowman, I can build a snowcow!"

"Huh?" Pig asked. "Who ever heard of a snowcow?"

But Cow was determined. She scooped together piles of snow and began to build. First she made four legs. Then she patted on more snow for the body.

"Ha ha ha!" Pig laughed as Cow finished. "Is that your idea of a cow? It looks more like a camel! You should know what a cow looks like, Cow!"

Cow stopped. "Maybe I should have started with something simpler," she said, standing back from her work. Then she got an idea. "I know!" she said. "I'll build a snowman just like the children did!"

Her first try didn't look right, so she started over. Determined, she did better on the second try, but the snowman still needed some work. Cow began again. Each snow figure began to look better than the last.

Pig noticed lights glowing back at the barn. "It's almost time for the big Christmas party," he said.

"Go on ahead," Cow said, distracted by her work. "I want to finish this first."

"Hurry," Pig said over his shoulder. "You won't want to miss the Christmas party, the biggest, most important thing in the barn all year!"

That's when Cow got an idea . . .

Back in the barn, shiny decorations sparkled. The Farmer had covered the stalls in twinkling colored lights, then passed out special treats to all the animals. Everyone sang and laughed, played games and told stories.

"But where is Cow?" Goat wondered.

"I guess she hasn't come in yet," said Pig.

The party went ahead without Cow. Everyone took turns telling what Christmas meant to them.

"Enjoying my family and friends all together!" Chicken said.

"Yummy Christmas food!" Goat cried.

"All-night parties!" Horse hollered.

"Presents, presents, and more presents!" Pig shouted.

Presents! Every year the animals gathered to exchange the gifts that they carefully prepared for one another.

"But what about Cow?" asked Goat. Horse yelled out the barn door, "Come in, Cow! You're missing Christmas!"

"Soon," Cow shouted. "I'll be there soon."

"We might as well start!" Horse hollered.

"Who is going to start?" Sheep asked.

"Me! Me! Me!" Pig yelped, dashing toward the pile of gifts. "I want to give the first gift!" He reached into the pile. "This is from me to my good friend Chicken!" He excitedly handed Chicken the package, egging him, "Open it! Open it! OPEN IT!"

"Oh, thank you, Pig!" Chicken
said. He tore open the paper
and looked inside the box.
Everyone got very quiet. "Oh,"
Chicken said and pulled out a
scarf . . . exactly . . . like . . .
the one . . . Pig wore.
   "Isn't it great?!"
Pig said, dancing.

"Thank you!" Chicken said. He wrapped the scarf around his skinny chicken neck. "Thank you very much!" The scarf was much too big for Chicken, but he loved it just the same because Pig gave it with such joy.

The other animals opened their presents, laughing and joking between each one. Occasionally they took turns yelling out the barn window to Cow.

"Come in, Cow!"

"Come enjoy the party!"

Cow answered each call the same way: "I'll be there soon."

Soon came, and just one present waited to be opened.
"It's Cow's!" cried Goat. "She's missing
everything!"

"Let's all go outside and get her," Horse said.

"But it's so cold out there," Sheep fretted.

"Let her stay outside and freeze if she wants," Pig said. "She is missing what Christmas is all about: being together with family and friends, eating great food, telling fun stories, and getting presents—celebrating!"

The more Pig talked, the more upset he became. "Well, if that silly Cow won't come in here to celebrate Christmas, I'll go out there and get her myself!" he huffed.

"Me too!" Goat said.

All the other animals followed. The party would not be complete without Cow! Up the hill they paraded.

Cow didn't even notice. She worked away, patting snow here, smoothing snow there.

"Cow!" Pig said. "Please come to the Christmas party. It just isn't the same without you!"

Cow kept working. "I'm almost finished," she announced. "See, I've made an entire scene in the snow. I'm calling it 'The Spirit of Christmas.'"

"The what?" Pig asked.

"Oh!" Sheep exclaimed. "That's beautiful, Cow." Sheep pointed to a trough made from snow. "Look! A manger, like the one where Jesus was born! Oh, and look over there—wise men!"

"What?" the animals asked.

"Sure!" Sheep said. "This shows the real meaning of Christmas." The animals leaned closer as she said, "Nearly two thousand years ago, Jesus was born in a manger . . ."

"What's a manger?" interrupted Chicken.

"It's that thing we eat from every day," Horse whispered.

"Not me," Chicken said. "I never eat from a manger."

"Some of us do," Horse replied.

Pig wondered aloud, "It just isn't right—"

"Sure it is!" Goat interrupted. "You eat from one too."

"No, no, no," Pig squealed. "I mean it just doesn't seem right that Jesus was born in a crummy old manger. He should have been born in a huge palace!"

"But that's the way God chose to do it!" Sheep said. "He didn't need a lot of money or an expensive place to live. He came to us for Christmas! He came to live right where we are, just like us!"

All Cow's friends thought about what Christmas really meant. Chicken thought about enjoying family and friends all together. Goat thought about all the yummy holiday food. Horse thought of all-night parties. Pig thought about presents, presents, and more presents! Suddenly they each knew Christmas was more than these things, much more. It was about receiving what God gave with great joy—and receiving Jesus right here, right now.

Cow stood back from her hushed friends and studied her snow scene. "It seems to be missing something," she said.

"What could be missing?" Pig wondered. "There's the manger, and here are the wise men, and there are Mary and Joseph . . ."

"That's it!" Cow said. "We are missing!"

"Yes," Sheep said, smiling. "The manger scene is not complete without us—we are part of it!"

So Christmas came, right there, right then . . . and everyone took a closer look at the spirit of Christmas.